CYSCOPRIME
PUBLISHERS

Cyscoprime Publishers

An Imprint of Evincepub Publishing
Parijat Extension, Bilaspur, Chhattisgarh 495001
First Published by Cyscoprime Publishers 2020
Copyright © Rasha Hameed 2020
All Rights Reserved.
ISBN: 978-93-90047-14-7

THE NEGLECTED ONE

Rasha Hameed

About The Book

"THE NEGLECTED ONE" is a collection of poetry and prose by Rasha Hameed. The collection is about survival. It is divided into sections, with each section serving a different purpose and relevance to the life experiences of the untold heroes. The sections explore the themes of violence, abuse, love, loss, and femininity. The collection delves into all the various aspects and emotions that come with falling in love. The heartache when it ends, the butterflies when it's new, the abuse experienced in some relationships. Along with it the author also presents the dark side of society and relationships.
The book is divided into 4 series: the eternal series", "the dark series", "the mystery series " and "the crown series".

This collection discusses personal trauma that is recommended for the ages of 14 and up.

The "Dark Series" is so devastating you wonder if you will survive. The narrative tells of the pain of loss and the elation of triumph, capturing in finely wrought detail the experience of being a young woman in today's world.
Whereas the last section , "The Crown Series" completely contrasts the "Dark Series". In this section, the poems' themes focus on a hopeful determination to rise above difficulty and discouragement. By turns fearless and intimate this section will strengthen your soul and inspire you to celebrate your own experience. Overall through this collection, she tries to capture complex feelings and emotions in a way that is easily digestible and will be rooted forever in your heart.

About The Author

Rasha Hameed is pretty much an ambiverted poet wrapped up in her parallel universe. Most of the time she's pretty much engrossed in researching about the universe and technology. Besides poetry, Rasha is passionate about Football, Portrait Sketching and Coding.

She is pursuing her under grad engineering degree from Mangaluru, India. Rasha was inspired by Shakespeare's works, which was the reason she says she was drifted towards poetry. There's always a story to tell when you are with her.

Contents

Rasha Hameed

THE ETERNAL SERIES

Rasha Hameed

I will detach detach your sorrows,
Through the perfect bliss.
I will shade your love,
Through the honored oath.
I will destroy your darkness,

Through the eternal light.
I will fill your emptiness,
Through the in toxic wine.
I will kill your fear,
Through the truth too dear.

So I ask you to be mine,
And make my other half divine

.

They made it clear,
They'll stay forever.
Just like the salt and the
sweet water
Miraculous enough not
to mix with each other

And hold on tight my dear,
For the fireflies are embracing the night
For the moon is kissing the ocean
For the stars are disintegrating into stardusts And
you my dear Is on the verge to steal my heart...

The supernova I see in your eyes:
Wild enough to destroy everything
Yet
Beautiful enough to die for....

Girl's POV:
Seven years pass by,
My eyes meet those hazel eyes,
Which once left my heart impaired.
The feeling of butterflies in my stomach,
Once again, after a long pause of Seven years:
Can it be that it is he?

 Boy's POV:
The woman who was once a dream,
Stood in front of me.
My heart skipped a beat.
For I know not why...
The electrifying touch sensed Seven years ago

Was still running over my body...

Yes it is she!

8

THE DARK SERIES

<u>THE PERFECTLY IMPERFECT ILLUSION</u>

With full of darkness all around,
This is only what my eye absorbs
I needn't need to give you a source for this
For you already know what's more focused in my
heart's core...

As much as the seven seas apart our bodies lie,
But still our heart's chained, even when the soul dies.
Under the sky of moonlit night;
Like dreamers we lie, feeling both the beautiful and
the dark night...

Though millions of stars you gaze,
You are only what I see, because you are situated in
my heart's base.

With every new obstacle our life slits,
A new chapter unfolds;
From here begins a new era for us....
An era that brings forth immortality....

Staring at you all a time,
Did my brain detect your every cell;
Neither was it the extrasensory perception within me,
Nor the code can I predict for your mesmerizing eyes,
But merely the chemistry between us....

I came to know I'd stopped breathing,
Being two inches away from you.
How crazy it is, that every day I crave for your touch,
But it is your love that leaves me numb....

Standing under the moonlight,
Sensing the cool sand, being barefooted,
Like men of old,
Did we feel every comfort of it...

Under the silence of twilight,
As the bioluminescent waves clash our feet;
Holding hands, bringing the tingling effect,
But all these remain an illusion just perfect;

Time passed ,
People changed,
But my heart's still,
Awaiting for you to fill;
My heart in the same path, but you turned away;
Now it's lost nowhere,
Chasing your illusion everywhere......

<u>ABANDONED DIARY</u>

Dear diary,
This letter is for the person, I most admire about,
Whose every moment my eye catches,
For the first person who comes into my mind when I
open my eyes
And the last person whom I sense in my dreams

My chapters had always
been incomplete without your existence
You are the fundamental unit of my life
My love towards you is immeasurable
Believe it or no, but its greater than the attraction
between nucleus and electrons.

My first sight on you, made my heart leap,

Your every word froze my nerves,
Your every touch left my body electrified....

The thing I feared the most is Oblivion,
My soul was dead before your first step in my life
Your every tear became my greatest fear.

I didn't find the destiny of my life,
I chased it...
And it was you,
When my heart captured you,
I chased you ...

You always accompanied me to the path of eternity,
But only until those days came when you
transformed my nightmare to reality;

Bitter were those days when your heart resisted on
accepting me
Deadly were those days when I stopped chanting the
eight- lettered password...

Your were my drug,
You left me diseased instead of comfort...

Whenever my eye caught something of yours,
I wished the earth would swallow me.

Rasha Hameed
Every day I sensed the hallucination of being
immortal with you,
My journey started with you,
I timed you.
But now when the clock has stopped,

It all ends unexpectedly.
Lost souls headlines all over,
But just our body lies absorbed by the Earth...

<u>*HER POSESSION*</u>

I always asked him not for you,
For hatred was all that I needed,
Hope was never built in me,
Until he sent you…

I admit it, at times I've been rude to you,

But a tear from your eye would make me a raging beast…

You were not my option,
But my only choice,

Rasha Hameed
I never want to fail.

I tried hard to stay away from you,
For I was an incurable Viral disease,
But your immune,
Destroyed its signs too…

Judge me not for who I was,
For you wouldn't believe it.
Be not close to me,
For you will drown in the deep sea…

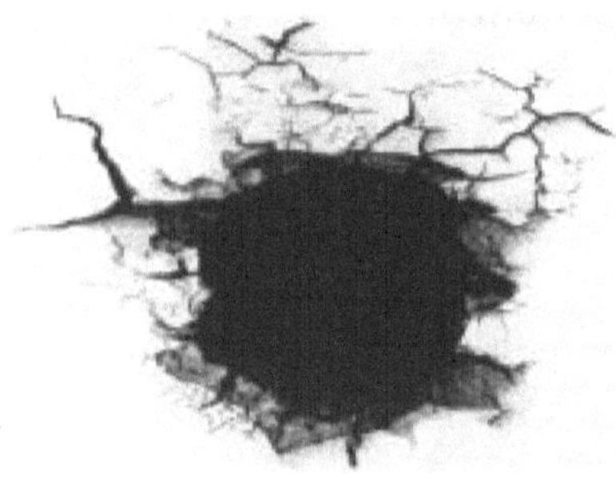

I won't say what my
verses mean,
For you know what I
convey.

Time will last, but the signs won't,
For you will not be able to see the face behind my
mask…

THE FATE'S TRAP

She asked this question over and over again:
'What life was?'
When her attempts never gave an answer,
She ended up leaping from the bridge…

The case, the rumors, the gossips,
Didn't last more than a month;
She was just long lost in all hearts.

It all started when she was 18
It all started because she was a girl!

Suicide?
They thought it was too cheap.
Giving no attempts from themselves to raise its worth...

They tagged her as a loser,
Confined within four walls.
They titled her a slut,
For hanging up with the opposite sex.
Not knowing her reality in depth.
She got popularized for the latest topic of gossip
An item for a sample...

Millions of dreams did revolve around her,

Born not for just mere imagination...

Destiny did challenge,
But life never gave her a chance to participate
How often did she drown in the sea of sadness?
None else than her soul would feel the pain;
How often was she being used for being too good?
None else than her heart would sense its intense…

She was caught in the fate's trap,
The one that seemed impossible to escape.

Her life began to retrograde.
Her heart and soul started giving reasons.
Dreams developed for shattering,
Finally breaking down her conscious,
Did she choose death over life

Rasha Hameed

THE CUT...

She let me get her into the root of my heart,
For the unstable root
needed something to penetrate.
My light was she,
For she illuminated the
path drowned in darkness.

The pulse in my vein,
Like the silent ocean;
The rain showering in my brain,
Like a creature under a rock unseen...

For I believed that flowers don't grow under a dry
earth,
For I knew seeds sprouts passing through harsh
weather,
For I saw the forests shade even the drunk man,
For now I see a hopeful present,
As she breaks the myth of dead heart never coming to
life…

For now,
Life had all shades,
As the bleeding heart cut being cut by many sharp
blades,
Had been band aid.

For now moments were like captured sunsets,
Where trust was never dim
And where,
Hatred will never swim…

<u>BODY NOT FOUND…</u>

I sit on the green grass,
Shining and reflecting under the natural light;
Do I gaze the saffron clouds,
Enjoying the last few hours of my soul's company.

Just a sheet of paper and topless pen,
Does the tragedy behind my smile unlocks then…

Placing the inky stick between my fingers,
Trembling as a tremor shook the paper.

The source all starts with a 'Hello'.
And terminates being lost.

One more glance it all read…

"Feb 29, 2000
The day which comes once in every four years,
But it'll come for me every day.
A nightmare which I thought just an illusion in
reality,
Did paralyze my heart forever.

Barely was I fourteen,
Did a devil harass me sexually,
He took away with him the joy;
After leaving my soul bloody.

Not to re read this chapter of my life again,
Did I zip my mouth
And stitch my heart
Thinking I would get a fucking new start...
But life was so lazy and selfish,
That it resumed the chapter adding new flavors.

Days passed like seconds,
But every second seemed like an hour.
Spending every minute replaying the chapter
In the corner of the dark room
Sensing nothing beside me.

Finally the day came,
When the man of my life stood besides my dad.

Having thought of him as his shadow,
Did I finally accept the proposal.

Thy heart misspelled restart for resume...
It didn't interact with the brain,
Neither did it allow the brain to interfere.

Being ignorant of this man's identity as my shadow
killer,
Did this decision pay a heavy fine for the rest of my
life.

A new woman all day under his pants,
Actually under whom I should be shielded.
But his act of shielding was just my mere imagination,
Beyond his act of fornication.

It was this flame that kept me all alive,
In the form of this small version of me.

But this devil was so unavoidable,
As evil was his birthright...
He chopped of this little one,
 This little flame of mine,
The one evolved from his own blood!

Five years ago,
He left my soul gory, leaving the stains unclean..."

Neatly folding this history
Do I place it inside a bottle,
To let it float and travel round the globe;
On the aim to let this world know my world...

Finally,
Stepping towards the majestic ocean,
Feeling the final greatness of it.

Rasha Hameed

Only a few inches for my final destination,
Do I lean near the cliff,
Gaping at its depth.
Did I finally manage to leap,
Tasting death…

FORCED...

"October 12, 2001"
You flashed by me,
My heart experienced a jerk,
Your name tightened my ribs,
I was desirous to continue
'Cause I was an adventure freak...

"November 12, 2001"
Staying hideous from the world
I watch you behind the screens
Hoping I wouldn't be seen.
But who knew you were so keen,
To complete your lust unseen.

"January 12, 2002"
You caused me to swallow,
A frozen illusion.
You left me wandering,
By spilling dark delusion.
For I knew you wouldn't stop with a conclusion.

"April 12, 2002"
The month proved me a halfwit
For I was mesmerized with the game
Thinking I still had saviors,
Thinking I killed the warriors,
But who knew that the warrior was the evil shadow carrier...

"August 12, 2002"
The bruises, the scars, the pains you drew,
The pool of blood, the gardens of darkness you implanted,
Disfigured my heart.
Discouraged my emotions.
Discolored my dignity.

"December 12, 2002"
Oh ,how I wish!
I could turn back the time .
Oh ,how I wish!
I didn't break my pieces.
Oh ,how I wish!
I'd never meet you.

"February 12, 2004"
Athens was carrying the history,
Dictatory executed for public satisfactory,
Disappearance in Bermuda still remained a mystery.
But my story still submerged
Under the ocean uncharged.

"July 12, 2004"
The beast inside you kept growing,
For it loved the sound of me growling.
The hell loved your choice of residence,
For you reverted the angels to demons in the process
of resurgence,
By your depiction of fake eminence.

"October 12, 2004"
Survival seemed like a challenge,
Living seemed like a desire,
Emotions seemed like a deadpan,
Hallucinations seemed like a drug,
And fleeing seemed like an impossible.

"January 12, 2005"
The scent of blood became my oxygen,
The scars became my birthmark,
Forced fornication became my morning tea,
Silence became my shadow.
And then,

Departing the soul became my only therapy.

"May 12, 2007"
I was covered in my own filth,
My hands were red spilled,
My veins were frozen with guilt.
'Cause I was in awe with my skill,
For I caused the evil to be killed.

"February 12, 2010"
Time passed as it was promised,
But the moment still frozen like today.
Scars appeared to heal,
Life progressed towards uphill.
But who knew ,
That deed would leave a black hole drill.

"December 12, 2012"
All eyes on me ,
A queen to fear.
All crowns on me,
An inspiration in fire.
All power within me,
A history in growth.

THE LAST NOTE

Dear Friend,
Our journey began by smiles and glances all day,
Resumed by mere exchange of numbers.
But,
Who knew , life was gonna bring forth a new part.
And here the story unfolds…

Travelling in the same compartment of life,
Never did we attempt to read each other's bio data.
Until, there came a day;
When I sensed that you are the last person alive on
earth…

Little did I try to pair up with you,
Not knowing, this minute mistake would change my
route.

All day long,
I did judge your life blindly.
Thinking it as normal and simple.
Being ignoramus of how badly you craved for this
simple life…

Your eyes said nothing was impossible for you;
But only until I studied your soul deeply,

Did I find what lay beyond my thoughts...

Your wrist marks,
Rumors spreading like sparks,
Gave folks reasons for a new narration.

How immature was I,
To believe we are gonna survive this adventure.
How fool was I,
To trust you, that you are gonna accompany me in
the ship of success,
Whereas you let yourself to harass you soul.

Now there I kneel,
Facing your clot less body,
Swallowed by Earth.

Numb,
But droplets from my eyes flowing copiously.
Heart torn apart,
I lay there for hours.
Cursing and murmuring myself like a lunatic,
For letting you go alone...

HALLUCINATING...

I never thought sharing the same domain would be my comfort,
I never thought your gags would build my mood,
I never thought your smile would make my day,
I never thought our parting would be this year's worst heartbreak.

Detention wouldn't have been hallucinating without you,
And definitely attendance would've been a shortfall for me, if it weren't you.

You told the story of the storms you survived,
Your words could become an aspiring book of mine.

I'll ache for the moments cherished with you,
I'll crave to get back the time spent with you.

And now comes the day,
When we can't stay together;
So bury me in your heart,
I'll heal you forever.

<u>THE PAIN…</u>

It hurts
walking on the earth without you
It hurts
 Hallucinating your voice
It hurts
Searching for your smile in others
 It hurts
Knowing that you are six feet below the earth

36

THE MYSTERY SERIES

37

Rasha Hameed

I felt the darkness behind me,
As if all ready to consume me.
The more swift my feet hiked,
The more was its intense majestic and psych...

Thy eyes
exploited to black,
And thy heart chained in shack...
All owed my breath,
'Cause it inhaled evil and death...

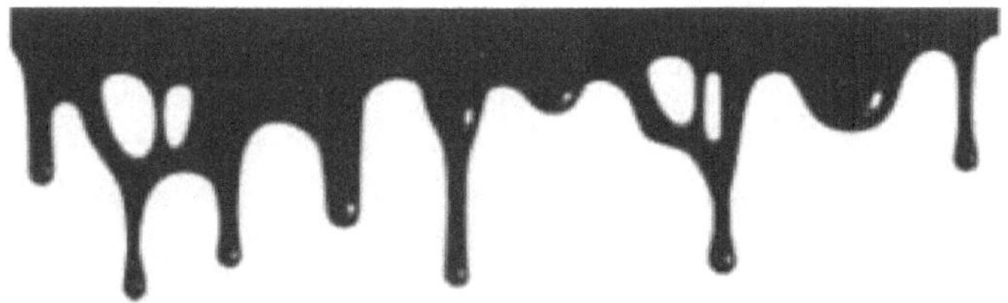

And as the sky dusked,
The moon yearned to meet the ocean.
The shadows got long and hard.
The Bioluminescence woke up to Life.
And secretly,
The crave for blood provoked the vampires.

She tried to be different,
For she knew all the fingerprints never matched.

She believed, in the world upside down,
For she battled with the demo dragons there.

She believed, the lost land of Atlantis,
Was never created.
For she saw the two faces of curiosity there.

Submerged in the blood of devil.
Soaked with the stains of evil.
Unleashing the beast's demand,
Lay another soul drowning with darkness,
Victimized by my cursed hands.

Rasha Hameed

I'm drooling
Over the stars
Over the Galaxy
And
Over the mediocre
Which doesn't exist

The ends sprinkling stardust in my veins
Keeping the aura, a mystery.
Leaving the remains jazzy
Just like the supernova glittery.

Rasha Hameed

We are so engrossed in building the mediocre,
Unconscious of how venturesome the real ride is...

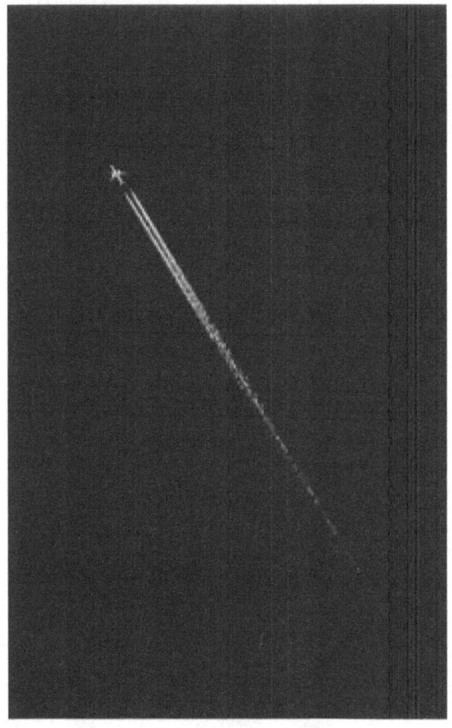

The arena of blood and war
The site of demons and dragons

The spot of fire and destruction
The city of arrogant and sinners
The country shielded with hellfire

It's thought brought shivers down my spine
Its interpretation filled my eyes with fear and
darkness
It's tale ripped my heart and froze my veins

History was repeating again

And this place was it,
Which left me wandering for years,
Which left my emotions punctured,
Which left my senses lost.

This voyage was just :
The desert I could see,
The Oasis I was in delusion with,
The thirst that just tortured me,
The heat that burnt my hope,
Until I found the ocean
And the wrecked ship
That was when I realized I was rightly guided.

And
The Sun and the moon have overlapped
The rays are woken from the west
 The stars are disintegrating
The mountains are crumbling
The seas have over flown
The infant is being killed
The children have turned white haired
Oh you!
How will you save yourself from such a day?

She wrapped herself with the bloodstained quilt,
For its scent,
Engrossed her in memories of her small creature,
For its scent,
Kept her alive ever minute.
For its scent,
Gave her hopes of departing the planet soon

She rouse from the grave
Compacted enough to crush her bones
Dark enough to be engulfed in fear.

Her eyes swollen like that of a regretful sinner,
Her dark circles carrying the weights of her deeds,
Her face blackened like that of a coal.

She could see,
The whole Humankind ever stepped on the planet,
Coursing to a locus, as if they were swarms of locusts,
She could see,
The sky above her like the face of tanned oil,
The mountains crumbling down sacrificing it's might,
The sun burying the moon,
The ocean drinking itself.
She could see,
Now came the time she was promised...

Scared to fall in love again?
Have you ever mused over;
The stars glaring over you,
So that you would bury your pain.
The moon staying overnight,
So that it could heal your wounds.
 And
The one waiting above the seven skies
So that you come back to him again...

Deep thoughts making me sober again
Once again Sprinkling stardust on my veins

Rasha Hameed

Are you not wondered?
How majestically he paints the sky!
Are you not wondered?
How flawlessly he structured your fingerprints!
Are you not wondered?
How gloriously he commands the universe!
Are you not wondered?
How exquisitely he partitioned the two seas!
Are you not wondered by his kingship?
So will you not reason?

I realized my heart was sunken in black,
Parallel to the lungs of Chain smokers.
I realized I wouldn't survive for too long,
For I perceived I was on the concluding stage.
So,
Now I exhale the shit and inhale the spirit,
For I discovered, it was the only chemotherapy that
would heal me...

The woods,
Dark and dragged out.
The ocean,
Deep and infinite.
And my soul,
Wandered and lost.

And the lost city of Pompeii
With it's perfectly preserved state
Rendered a narration of the past,
Held signs for the present,
Traversed a mystery for the future...

56

THE CROWN SERIES

Rasha Hameed

Your hazel eyes won't make me feeble,
Your false oaths won't leave me mesmerized,
Your perfect body won't infect my heart,
Your insecure threats won't pull me down,
Your futile power won't make me affordable,
'Cause I'm the Queen
In the underworld unseen..

Darling
It's just how you
Take it
Feel it
Transform it
Until you are someone
You are pleased with

Rasha Hameed

I find it Silly enough,
How you judge me by a piece of cloth
I find it absurd,
How every time you mock my intelligence
I find it insane,
How you sympathize me for being oppressed

For you won't know ,
That the crown was only bestowed to courageous
That the crown chose me to be its warrior
That the crown was a tribute for my strength and softness

So don't be jealous my dear,
For I was honored to wear it as I was potential enough to bear its heaviness

The arrow that never missed its target
Struck right into the core
Aching not just the flesh but also the ribs
The ages it took to heal
The therapy it took to discover
Just so that the pieces broken could mend once again
Giving birth to a new me evolving through those pieces again

I fell
But wasn't knocked out.
My knees wobbled
But I knew I had to be erect with ten toes.
There stood no one beside me
But hundreds following me
And one in the battlefield trying to overpower me .

My emotions
were restless,
But not my intelligence.
My arms were broken,
But not my hopes.
I knew I had to win this battle,
Till the last breath.
Till the last breath.
Till the last breath...

Heat waves rushing through my veins
Fire of hungry beast in my eyes
Urge to soak my hands in blood
All transformed
Into an unbeatable success

And if you ever ask me to describe a woman's greatness,
I would commence with the story of hundreds,
I would tell you the stories of:
The woman who stood resistant in front of a tyrant,
The woman who rebelled when the wicked tried to rip off her modesty,
The woman who abandoned her luxury for the hereafter...

If it wasn't for misery,
Would I be smeared by my scars?
If it wasn't for misery,
Would I be submerged in my nightmares?
If it wasn't for misery,
Would I be inflicted with poverty?
For if I wasn't stigmatized,
Would I be able to hold up the heaviness of my crown?

Rasha Hameed

I don't hold any grudge over failure,
For it taught me to embrace demons and turn them
into angels...

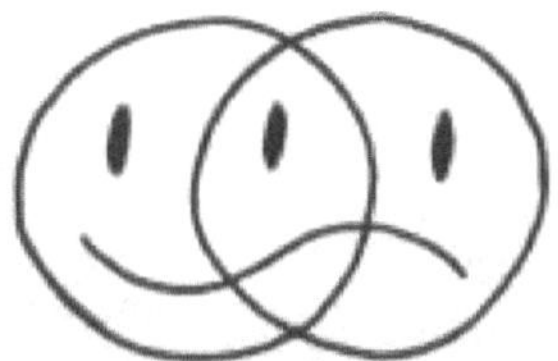

And I thought,
The luminosity would fade my darkness away,
But who knew,
Its intensity was so vigorous;
That at the end it'd only leave me blinded

And she knew,
The day would arrive,
When her dad would whistle for her in front of millions.

Yes, I was scared.
I was scared my words would kill people.
I was scared my words would bring darkness.
But only until,
I learned how to phrase them.

There's ,
Magic in her bitterness.
Force in her courage .
Fierce in her pride.
Wild enough,
To drive any beast supine.

Like the hopeful bulb that flickers,
Even when close to death…

So shall I burn with faith
When hatred is close to its end.

Did my meeting with her was a coincidence?
She's a woman almost impossible to tame with.
To tame her is as much as hard as to describe her…

A woman with a strong connection with God,
A woman with a crown that never droops,
A woman with a strong, yet, soft heart,
A woman brave enough to cut her past shadows,

A woman honored as the Mafia Queen….

AF415935

* 9 7 8 9 3 9 0 0 4 7 1 4 7 *